For all the summers in Newfoundland with Eric and Alice May
KC

For Gran and Grandad
MK

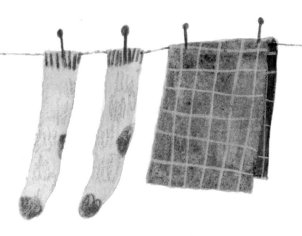

Text copyright © 2022 by Karla Courtney
Illustrations copyright © 2022 by Madeline Kloepper

First edition 2022

Library of Congress Catalog Card Number pending
ISBN 978-1-5362-1152-8

22 23 24 25 26 27 APS 10 9 8 7 6 5 4 3 2 1

Printed in Humen, Dongguan, China

This book was typeset in Bembo.
The illustrations were done in colored pencils and gouache and finished digitally.

Walker Books US
a division of Candlewick Press
99 Dover Street
Somerville, Massachusetts 02144

www.walkerbooksus.com

Poppy's House

Karla Courtney

illustrated by Madeline Kloepper

WALKER BOOKS

Sometimes I like to go to the island.

It's far beyond the end of the road
and across the foggy sea . . .

past icy mountains

and boats with loud horns

and
humpback whales
swimming with
the waves . . .

past wild forests
and painted houses
and docks piled with traps and dories.

On top of a hill, where the ocean shines on all sides,
sits a little yellow house.

This is where Poppy lives.

Poppy lives alone, but he is always busy.

He chops the wood,

he picks the cloudberries,

he catches the fish . . .

and he watches his world float by as he sits in front
of a huge supper plate of salt beef and pease pudding.

Every morning
we have bread
from the oven
for breakfast.

BUTTER

Then we make sure the house
is just right.

We tidy the kitchen,

dig up the potatoes,

and water the garden.

When our chores are done,
we get to explore the island together,
counting our favorite things.

We count masts.

We count cod.

We count tracks.

We count clothes.

We count rows.

We count stones.

And we count the waves as the sea dances
its slippery, silvery jig.

At the end of each day,
as we curl up on his worn velvet armchair,
we don't count the numbers on his clock.

When it's time to say goodbye,
tears cloud our eyes and sting our cheeks
and soak right through Poppy's itchy wool sweater.

And we count the days until we are together again.